I'm a Duck

To Christine Bunting,
Sloan Bunting,
and Glenn Bunting,
for everything
E. B.

To Mr. John D. Ertel,
the art teacher who rescued me
W. H.

Text copyright © 2018 by Eve Bunting
Illustrations copyright © 2018 by Will Hillenbrand

First edition 2018

Library of Congress Catalog Card Number pending
ISBN 978-0-7636-8032-9

17 18 19 20 21 22 TLF 10 9 8 7 6 5 4 3 2 1

Printed in Dongguan, Guangdong, China

This book was typeset in Hightower.
The illustrations were done in mixed media.

Candlewick Press
99 Dover Street
Somerville, Massachusetts 02144

visit us at www.candlewick.com

I'm a Duck

Eve Bunting   illustrated by WILL HILLENBRAND

CANDLEWICK PRESS

When I was just an egg, I'm told,
I left my nest and rolled and rolled.

My mother quacked a frightened quack

then dived in deep
and brought me back.

Now I'm a duck who's scared to go
in the pond or lake, and so
I cannot swim, and that is bad.
A landlocked duck is very sad.

My brothers, swimming in a line,
shout "Come on in. The water's fine."
But I might sink and end up drowned,
never ever to be found.

My friend Big Frog told me today,
"I promise that you'll be OK.
Just slide in fast; don't even think.
You're a duck, and ducks don't sink."

I take a walk beside the pond,
then waddle just a bit beyond
to talk to Owl, who's very wise,
and ask him, "What do you advise?"

He studies me. "Too-wit, too-woo!
Think about what you can do.
You're a duck. Use common sense
and try to get some confidence."

It's true, if I could know for sure
that I could swim I'd feel secure.
I'll find a puddle. It will be . . .

the perfect practice place for me.

I puddle-swim all day and night.
It's nice to swim by pale moonlight!
My mother brings me out a snack.
She dries my feathers, rubs my back.

The pond is waiting there below.
It's whispering, "Come on! Let's go."
But even though I'm well prepared,
I'm really, really, really scared.

Frog's sitting on his big flat stone.
"If you're afraid to try alone,
I'll hold your wing and dive in, too,
to make it easier for you."

"I'd love to have you
    help me through it,
but I'm the one
    who has to do it."

I pause, aquiver for a minute.

Then hold my beak and flop right in it.

My friends are joyous. Frog is, too.
Owl calls out, "Too-wit, too-woo!"
My mother's jumping up and down
and blowing kisses all around.

I'm swimming! Oh my gosh, I find
that ducks are perfectly designed!
I was wrong to ever think
a well-made duck like me could sink.

I do the backstroke. There are cheers
so loud they almost hurt my ears.
The other ducks shout, "Way to go!"
as I'm backstroking to and fro.

We swim together in a line.
We're doing absolutely fine.
No one says my stroke is strange
or asks if I will ever change.

Wasn't it fantastic luck
that I grew up to be a duck?